Little RED
AND THE
VERY HUNGRY
LiON

Alex T. Smith

This is Little Red and today she is going to be gobbled up by a lion.

This Lion.
Well, that's what he thinks is going to happen anyway...

One hot morning Auntie Rosie woke up covered in **spots**.

There was
only one
thing for it.

RING!RING!RING!RING!RING!

"Oh dear! Oh dear!" said
Little Red when she heard the news.
"I'll come right away!"

THE
LL-YOU-NEED
GENERAL STORE

SNIP-SNIP BARBER

BEST CUTS IN TOWN!

FRUIT
& VEG

SPOT
MEDICINE

FRESH
DOUGHNUTS

So she packed her
basket, waved
goodbye to her
daddy and
set off.

...over
the sleepy
crocodiles...

It was a long way to
Auntie Rosie's house.

Little Red walked under
the giraffes...

...and dashed past
the chattering
monkeys...

She crept around the termite mounds and under the leaping gazelles.

Then she caught a lift on an elephant...

...and wiggled her way around the **hippos** and **warthogs**...

...and waved hello to the **meerkats.**

Then she sat down for a rest in the shade of a shady tree.

And that's when the Lion arrived.

The Very Hungry Lion.

"Oh hello," purred the Lion,
"Where are you going?"

"To visit my auntie who is
covered in spots," said Little Red.

And in the time it took for his tummy
to rumble, the Very Hungry Lion
had cooked up a

Very

Naughty

Plan...

My Very Clever Plan

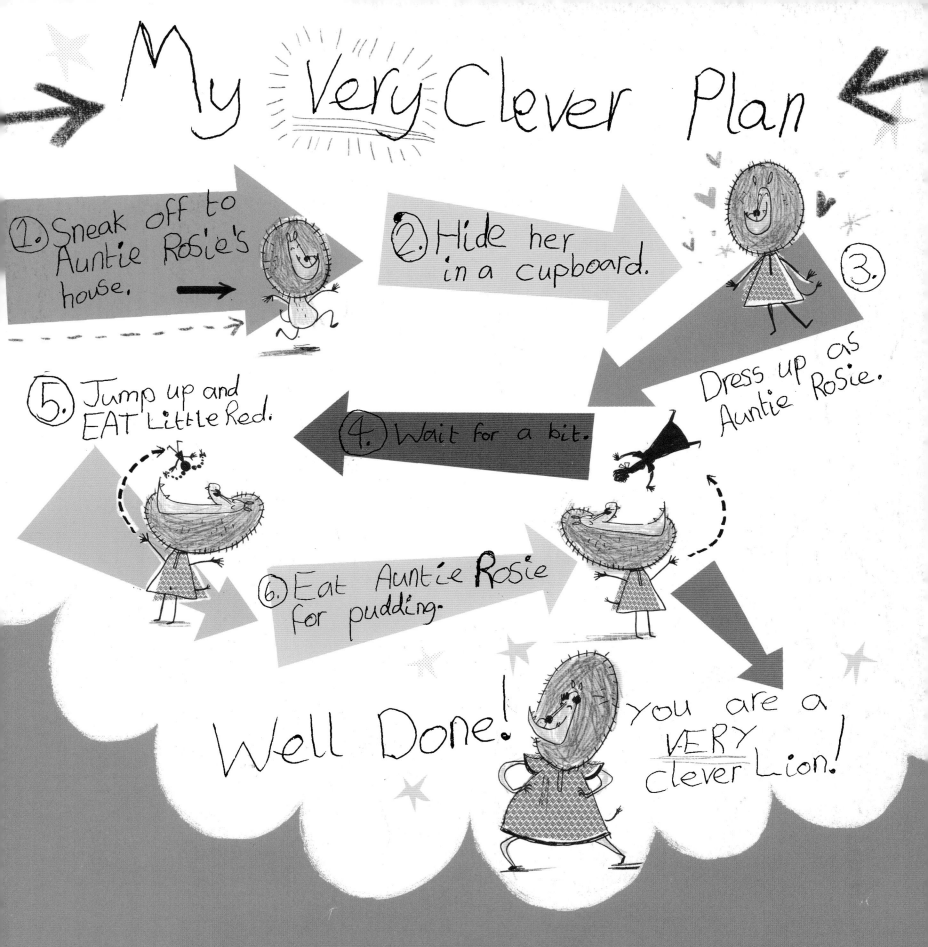

1. Sneak off to Auntie Rosie's house.

2. Hide her in a cupboard.

3. Dress up as Auntie Rosie.

4. Wait for a bit.

5. Jump up and EAT Little Red.

6. Eat Auntie Rosie for pudding.

Well Done! you are a VERY clever Lion!

And he rushed off to put his plan into action.

First, the Very Hungry Lion plonked Auntie Rosie in a cupboard and locked the door.

Then he squeeeeezed himself into one of her nighties and covered himself all over in spots.

Of course when Little Red arrived, she realised straight away it **wasn't Auntie Rosie** sitting in the bed.

She quickly looked around and spotted her auntie peeking through a gap in the cupboard.

Then Little Red decided that she was going to teach the naughty Lion a **lesson!**

"Oooh Auntie!" cried Little Red,
"What tatty hair you have!"

And before the Very Hungry Lion
could even lick his lips, Little Red...

...had brushed

and combed...

...and
twisted
and
braided
until the Lion had
a
lovely
new look.

This had **not** been in the Lion's plan.

So...

...he opened his mouth wide and...

"Blimey!" tutted Little Red.

"What grubby, grotty teeth you have, Auntie!"

And Little Red made
the Very Hungry Lion
brush,
brush,
brush
his teeth until
they sparkled.

"Oh Auntie!" sighed Little Red,
"What an old **nightie** you are wearing!"

And before the Very Hungry Lion
knew it, Little Red had
found him a **much**
prettier frock
to wear.

This had **not** been in the
Lion's plan either...

STOP!

yelled the Lion.

"I am a Very Hungry Lion

and my tummy is grumbly!"

The Very Hungry Lion let Auntie Rosie out of the cupboard and said SORRY ever so politely.

Little Red waggled a finger.

"Well, trying to gobble up children and poorly aunties is VERY naughty. If your tummy was rumbly, all you had to do was ask nicely for some food."

Then the three of them munched through a basketful of **doughnuts** together.

(The Lion had **five**.)

Soon it was beginning to get dark, so the Lion walked all the way back home with Little Red on his **very** best behaviour, and he promised to **never, ever, ever** try to eat another auntie **or** any children.

But he **might** be tempted to **eat a Daddy!**